Ellie's Magical Bakery

Brilliant Birthday Bakes!

ELLIE SIMMONDS

Illustrated by Kimberley Scott

RED FOX

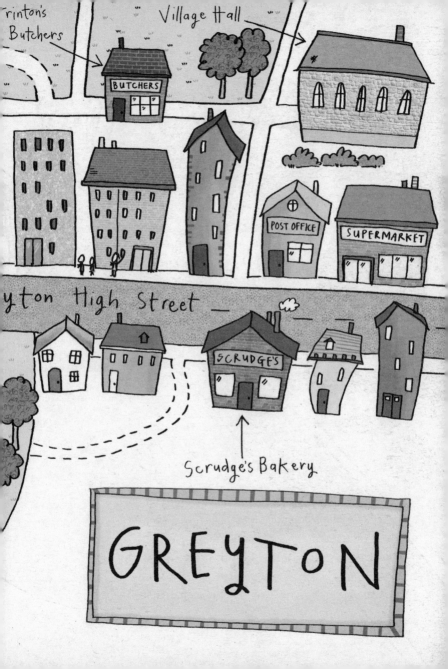

This book belongs to:

Write your name here

Draw your picture here

With special thanks to Lil Chase

Ellie's Magical Bakery: BRILLIANT BIRTHDAY BAKES!
A RED FOX BOOK 978 1 782 95268 8

First published in Great Britain by Red Fox,
an imprint of Random House Children's Publishers UK
A Penguin Random House Company

Penguin
Random House
UK

This edition published 2015

1 3 5 7 9 10 8 6 4 2

Penguin Random House is committed to a sustainable future for our business, our readers
and our planet. This book is made from Forest Stewardship Council® certified paper.

MIX
Paper from
responsible sources
FSC® C016897

Red Fox Books are published by Random House Children's Publishers UK,
61–63 Uxbridge Road, London W5 5SA

www.**randomhousechildrens**.co.uk
www.**totallyrandombooks**.co.uk
www.**randomhouse**.co.uk

Addresses for companies within The Random House Group Limited
can be found at: www.randomhouse.co.uk/offices.htm

THE RANDOM HOUSE GROUP Limited Reg. No. 954009

A CIP catalogue record for this book is available from the British Library.

Printed and bound in Great Britain by CPI Group (UK) Ltd, Croydon CR0 4YY

Chapter 1

Ellie looked down at her shopping list.

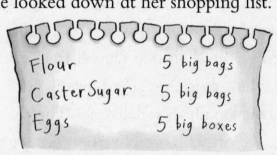

Flour	5 big bags
Caster Sugar	5 big bags
Eggs	5 big boxes

Ellie's Magical Bakery had only been open for a few weeks, but the shop was doing well. Ellie and her best friend, Basil,

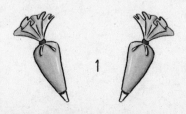

had a daily routine: in the morning Ellie would open up and get ready for the day ahead, baking some more fabulous treats for the villagers of Greyton. Their magical friend Victoria Sponge would help her, while Basil served the customers. Even Ellie's cat, Whisk, would lend a paw. He loved the delicious smells in the bakery.

After the shop had closed, they cleaned the whole place, prepared for the next day, and then made their deliveries. They always finished off with a nice refreshing swim.

But on Friday afternoons, swimming came later. First they went shopping at Mr Contee's grocery shop.

"Do you think that's everything, Basil?" Ellie asked her friend.

He scratched his head thoughtfully, making his hair stand up on end. "I think so," he said. He had dark hair and glasses, and every day he wore a T-shirt with a picture of a different animal. Today's had a crab on it.

Basil lowered his voice to a whisper. "Why don't you check with *you know who*?"

Whisk miaowed. He loved it when *you know who* came out of her hiding place.

Ellie checked up and down the aisles of the shop. No one was around. So she took her magical recipe book out of the trolley and opened it. On the very first page there was a drawing of a woman with

tiny golden wings. She looked like a fairy, but instead of a crown, a pretty dress and a magic wand, she had a chef's hat, a white apron and a wooden spoon.

"Victoria Sponge . . ." Ellie whispered.

Just saying the words worked some sort of spell, and the little baker peeled out of the book, then flew up into the air, leaving a trail of glitter behind her.

"Hi," she said. "Do you need my help?"

Whisk jumped up on his hind legs to say hello.

"Yes please, Victoria Sponge," Ellie

replied. "We've already got flour, sugar and eggs for the bakery. Do you think we'll need anything else?"

Victoria Sponge floated around Ellie's head, making her long brown hair fly up. "I have a feeling that you might need some cucumbers too," she said with a smile. "*Lots* of them!"

That seemed a bit strange. Ellie didn't know any cake recipes that used cucumber, but when Victoria Sponge gave instructions, there was usually a reason for it. The magical baker hid herself in Basil's collar, and they headed off towards the vegetable section.

The cucumbers were on the highest shelf, so Basil said, "Don't worry, Ellie. I'll get it for you."

Ellie had a condition called achondroplasia, which meant that her arms and legs were shorter than most people's.

Basil stood on tiptoe, grabbed as many cucumbers as he could and passed them to Ellie to add to the other things in the trolley.

"And that's the shopping done!" said Ellie.

They paid Mr Contee for their items and headed back onto the high street. Mr Patel waved to her from across the road.

Before Ellie's Magical Bakery opened, Greyton had been a grey, miserable place to live. Now it was a much brighter, happier village.

As they walked along carrying the heavy shopping bags, Basil asked Ellie, "Will we have to close the shop early tomorrow – to make sure our costumes are ready and we arrive on time?"

"Arrive *where* on time?" she wondered.

Basil instantly turned pink. "Talia's birthday party," he said. "The invitation was very fancy – written in golden writing. Didn't you get one?"

Ellie shook her head. She definitely would have remembered an envelope with golden writing.

"Sorry, Ellie," Basil said. "I was sure Talia would have invited you too."

Talia had come into the shop with her parents lots of times. Now that Ellie ran the bakery, she knew most people in the village, but she hadn't got many friends apart from Whisk – and now Basil, of

course. She had never been to a birthday party before.

Ellie felt very sad but she tried hard not to show it. "That's OK, Basil," she said. "Talia can't invite *everyone* to her party."

Whisk rubbed up against Ellie's legs to comfort her.

"Ellie!" came a voice from behind them. "Ellie! Wait! Please stop!"

When Ellie turned round, she saw a girl

running along the high street, waving at her. She had dark hair cut into a fringe, dark eyes and olive skin. It was Talia.

"Wowweee, Talia!" Basil said when she caught up with them. "We were just talking about you."

Talia smiled. "Were you talking about my party?" she asked with a grin.

Ellie smiled and nodded shyly.

"I'm very excited." Talia was speaking very quickly. "It's a garden party, and we're all going to dress up as either knights or princesses, and there's going to be a bouncy castle. We'll be using a china teapot and fancy cups and saucers, just like

the Queen! There will even be a butler taking everyone's invitations as they come in."

It sounded wonderful. "You could have cucumber sandwiches," Ellie suggested.

Talia clapped her hands in delight. "Like for afternoon tea!" she said. "My favourite!"

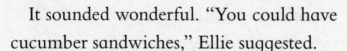

"I love afternoon tea too," Ellie said in a low voice. Because, of course, she wouldn't be eating cucumber sandwiches at Talia's party with the other guests.

They were interrupted by the ringing of a bicycle bell. Ellie turned just in time to see her horrible cousin, Colin Scrudge, riding along on his bike. He was holding a water pistol.

"Shrimp!" he shouted, which was the mean name he always used for Ellie. He pointed the water pistol at her.

"Duck!" she yelled to the others.

Ellie ducked, and Whisk ducked, and Talia ducked, but Basil didn't manage to duck in time. He got squirted right in the face.

"Ha ha ha!" Colin laughed. "That's what you get for hanging around with a stupid shrimp." Then he quickly rode away before they could say anything back.

Ellie scowled at him. Talia tutted. Whisk hissed.

"Are you OK, Basil?" Ellie asked.

Basil grinned. "The joke's on him! We're about to go swimming anyway so I don't mind getting a bit wet!"

Ellie smiled at him. She loved the way her friend was always so positive!

Talia turned to her. "Anyway, Ellie," she said. "I can't believe I forgot! I need to ask you something . . ."

Basil shot Ellie a look that said, *I told
you so*.

Ellie's hopes rose. Maybe Talia *had*
meant to invite her to the party after all!

Talia brushed her fringe out of her eyes.
"Would you be able to make me a cake,
please?" she asked.

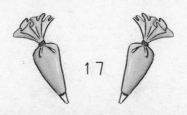

17

Ellie's face fell. Visions of children dressed as knights and princesses, sipping tea and eating cucumber sandwiches, vanished. She wondered if she would ever be invited to a party.

"I wouldn't go near the cakes at the Scrudges' bakery," Talia continued. "Their shop is *filthy*. But your cakes are the best for miles!"

Ellie felt proud. Even if Talia didn't like *her*, she liked her *cakes*, and that was something.

"I would be honoured to make the cake for your birthday party." She gave a low curtsey like she was addressing a real

princess. "M'lady."

Talia giggled. "Thank you so much, Ellie!" she said.

Ellie smiled. She couldn't go to the party, but she would bake Talia a brilliant birthday cake. The most brilliant cake that had ever been baked.

Chapter 2

Ellie came back from her evening swim and set to work planning Talia's cake. She had to wipe the dining table carefully

before she could put her magical recipe book on it. The Scrudges' flat wasn't much cleaner than their bakery below.

"Have you got a napkin?" Colin yelled over the noise from the TV.

"Just wipe your hands on the armchair," his mother yelled back.

Yuck, thought Ellie.

Ellie had once shared the flat above the bakery with her dad. But when he died,

her aunt and uncle Scrudge had moved in to take care of Ellie and run the shop. Unfortunately, they didn't do a very good job of either. They were mean to Ellie, and the bakery downstairs – which had once been filled with smells of yummy baking and tasty treats – had become as stinky as a swamp.

Ellie needed to concentrate. Whisk jumped up onto her lap and she opened the magical recipe book at the first page.

"Victoria Sponge . . ." she whispered.

The little baker winked at her from the page.

"I need to find the perfect recipe for

Talia's birthday party tomorrow," Ellie was very quiet. "It's a princesses-and-knights party . . . But I can't concentrate with all this noise."

"Just do your best, Ellie," said Victoria Sponge. "It's all you can ever do."

This was something Ellie's dad used to say to her too.

"Flick through the book and see what you can find," Victoria Sponge suggested.

Many of the pages at the front of the book had already been filled. There were *Pastries for a picnic*, *Sandwiches for a sunny Saturday*, *Buns for playing board games* . . . and many more. But at the back of the book, the pages were blank.

Victoria Sponge reappeared on each page as Ellie turned it.

"I'm not sure anything here is quite

right . . ." Ellie said.

"Look again," Victoria Sponge told her. "Maybe this time you'll find it."

"There's nothing—" Ellie suddenly stopped as she saw something moving across a blank page. All at once words started to appear, wiggling across the book like worms. As they formed, glittery dust puffed up into the air. Whisk tried to catch the dust on his tongue.

Ellie quickly looked over at her aunt and uncle, who were sprawled on the sofas.

25

Luckily their eyes were glued to the TV. When she looked down again, a brand-new recipe was written out in full.

"Look, Ellie!" Victoria Sponge grinned. Her wings fluttered on the page.

The recipe was called:

A brilliant bake for a brilliant birthday

Ellie gasped. It was just the recipe she was looking for!

"What are you doing over there?" Mrs Scrudge yelled. "You're putting me off my pizza." As she spoke, bits of food flew out of her mouth.

Colin craned his neck to see what was going on too. "She's reading a book," he sneered. "Why can't you just be normal and watch TV? Why would you want to read a book?"

Ellie shook her head. *What a silly thing to say!* she thought. She ignored her cousin

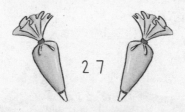

and studied the recipe. She would need eggs, flour, sugar, baking powder, cocoa powder . . . and, of course, a spoonful of Victoria Sponge's magical baking dust.

"What's that stupid thing you're reading anyway?" asked Mrs Scrudge; she couldn't heave her hefty body up off the sofa to come and see.

"It's a recipe book." Ellie shut the book quickly. "I'm pretty sure it belonged to my dad," she added. Up until now she had kept it a secret from the Scrudges, but she was proud to have it – and proud of

her bakery, no matter what they said.

"Pah!" said Mrs Scrudge. "Using a book is cheating."

"We never use recipe books," said Mr Scrudge. "I've never looked at a book in my life!"

And look how your cakes turn out, thought Ellie.

"It's not cheating," she explained. "It's taking advice. Sometimes I base a dish on a particular recipe but then make my own

29

additions, like using a different flavouring, or a different icing – or adding chocolate." She loved chocolate.

"Chocolate and sugar and all those ingredients are too expensive," said Mr Scrudge. "I use things I find around the house."

Hearing this, Whisk sounded like he was choking on a fur ball.

"All I care about is whether my customers like my cakes," said Ellie. "And they do. They come back every day to buy more."

"Probably because they feel sorry for you," muttered Mrs Scrudge. "Because you're so small and stupid."

Mr Scrudge got up and scratched his head. Flakes of dandruff sprinkled down all over his shirt. "Now, now," he said to his family. "Let's not be so hard on little Ellie."

Ellie's mouth fell open in surprise.

Whisk's jaw dropped.

Even Colin and Mrs Scrudge looked amazed.

Mr Scrudge was never nice to her. He was never nice to *anyone*.

Ellie held Whisk close. "What is he up to?" she whispered in his ear.

Whisk miaowed back in puzzlement.

"Ellie, dear," Mr Scrudge said, in a phoney-sounding voice. "Something came in the post for you last week."

Ellie leaped down from her chair, sending Whisk flying. She never got any post! "What? When? Where is it?"

"It was a fancy envelope with gold writing," he replied.

Ellie almost jumped up and down with delight. Basil had said that Talia's invitations had gold writing! Maybe Talia

had sent her one after all.

"*Dad!*" Colin groaned. "Why did you have to tell her?"

"Where is it?!" Ellie exclaimed.

"I put it somewhere safe," said Mr Scrudge. "In Colin's room."

"Oh, Dad!" Colin whined again.

Ellie didn't think this sounded like a very safe place at all – in fact, she'd been inside Colin's room before and it was a serious health risk. But she quickly dashed along the corridor to find her letter.

Colin's room was a mess – a very smelly mess, and even worse than she

remembered. There were clothes strewn everywhere, along with plates of mouldy, half-eaten food, and it smelled of stinky-cheese feet.

Ellie held her nose as she raced around, throwing clothes in the air, trying to find her letter. Whisk kept his distance by the door.

Finally she saw an envelope sticking out from underneath a mug on Colin's bedside table. When she pulled it out, it had a coffee ring on it, but it also had golden writing – and inside was the invitation she had been hoping for!

The fancy joined-up writing said

Dear Ellie,

– except that Colin had crossed out Ellie's name and added his own.

Dear ~~Ellie~~ Colin,

Princess Talia cordially invites you to attend her Royal Garden Party, on Saturday at 3 p.m.

Please bring this invitation to show to the butler on arrival as only princesses and knights will be admitted.

Then someone – presumably Talia – had written:

Hope you can make it, Ellie!

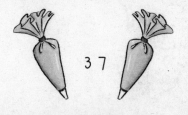

Ellie hugged the invitation to her chest. Talia *did* want her at her party – not just to make a cake. Ellie swore to herself that it would be the best cake she had ever made.

And now she had to come up with an outfit too!

Ellie's mind began to race with ideas for her costume. She couldn't believe it – tomorrow she'd be going to her very first birthday party!

Chapter 3

The next morning Ellie laid out her costume for the party on her bed. She had decided to go as a medieval knight. She'd found some cardboard at the back of the bakery storeroom, and covered it with tin foil to make a suit of shining armour. Her sword was a ruler wrapped in more foil. Luckily, in a bakery, there was loads of

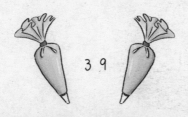

tin foil around. Ellie had even designed her own royal crest – the letters "EMB" written over a cupcake. She cut out the crest and stuck it on the front of her shield.

Even though she'd been up late making her costume, she was awake early this morning. There was lots to do before Talia's party.

"Come on, Whisk," she said to her cat as he stretched and yawned. She still needed to open the shop and make Talia's cake. "Now, where's my magical recipe book . . ."

Ellie scanned the room, and even though it was much tidier than Colin's, she couldn't see the book. She checked on her chest of drawers, under her bed,

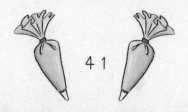

inside her wardrobe . . .

"Where did I last have it?" she asked Whisk.

Whisk miaowed, which wasn't much of an answer.

Ellie tried the kitchen, the living room, Colin's bedroom, and even the Scrudges' disgusting bakery . . . But even though she looked through all the mouldy food, dirtying her hands on all the mucky surfaces, she still couldn't find it.

"I wonder if Victoria Sponge took it back to my bakery . . ." she said aloud.

Whisk tilted his head on one side and raised a furry eyebrow, unconvinced. But

42

Ellie hurriedly got dressed and ran out onto the high street – and found that it was raining.

"Oh dear!" she said as she and Whisk ran as fast as they could to avoid getting too wet. This wasn't brilliant weather for a brilliant birthday. She hoped Talia's garden party wouldn't have to be cancelled.

Ellie's bakery was the smallest shop on the high street. It had a counter at the front so that they could serve passers-by, but now the shutters were down, waiting to be opened.

Basil was also waiting in the doorway, huddling with a few eager customers who were sheltering from the rain.

"Where have you been?" he asked.

"Sorry I'm late!" Ellie unlocked the front door. "Give me five minutes and I'll be ready," she told the customers.

Once inside, she started searching again straight away. The book was nowhere to be seen.

"I can't find the magical recipe book," she told Basil.

"Oh dear!" He frowned, then put on an apron which covered up the zebra on his T-shirt. "Have you asked Victoria Sponge if she knows where it is?"

Ellie shook her head, suddenly realizing something. "Victoria Sponge was *in the book!*

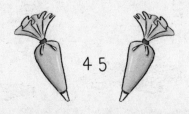

That means she's gone missing with it!"

"Wowweee," said Basil. "That really *is* a problem."

Ellie had climbed up onto the little stepladder she used, and checked her shelves, but the book wasn't there. She looked around her bakery, wondering if her bird's-eye view would help her spot it.

There was still no sign of it.

"What am I going to do?" Ellie wondered aloud. "I need to make the brilliant cake for Talia's birthday, but time is running out."

Basil cleaned his glasses on his apron.

"First things first," he said. "I'll open up the shop."

"OK," Ellie agreed with a nod. "We can start by selling the food we prepared last night."

Basil went over to the fridge and pulled

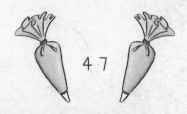

out some trays of cookies and cakes, taking them into the shop.

Ellie jumped down off the stepladder and helped him open the shutters.

"Come in out of the rain!" she said to the customers.

The queue of people hurried in gratefully, brushing the drops of rain off their coats.

"But how am I going to make the cake for Talia's birthday without the book?"

Whisk wound himself round Ellie's legs. She reached down and stroked his ears.

"Umm . . ." Basil thought for a minute. "What would Victoria Sponge say if she was here?"

Ellie knew the answer straight away. "She'd say, *Just do your best*. It's what my dad always said too."

Whenever Ellie thought of her dad, she was suddenly surrounded by the aroma of freshly baked cakes. Now she remembered his ginger beard, round cheeks and silly, deep chuckle, and instantly felt a little better.

"Well then!" Basil said. "What are you waiting for?" He turned to the first customer – Mr Contee from the grocery

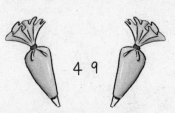

4 9

shop. "What can I get for you today, Mr C?"

Basil's positive attitude cheered Ellie even more and she got to work on Talia's cake.

She tried to remember the list of ingredients from the recipe that had appeared in the book the day before. She cracked two eggs into a bowl. Then she added flour, baking powder and sugar . . . but what else? The only other ingredient she could remember was Victoria Sponge's magical baking dust – but of course Victoria Sponge was the only person who had that, and she was missing, along with the book. Ellie hoped the little baker was OK. She couldn't believe she'd been so careless and lost her book.

There was another ingredient in the recipe, she just knew it . . . But she couldn't remember what it was.

While she thought about this, Ellie started making some more food for the shop. She wouldn't be able to use the ovens – not without Victoria Sponge's help – but she remembered some recipes she had tried before; ones that didn't need cooking.

She melted chocolate in the microwave and made some cornflake cakes. She got together some rocky road mix and pressed it into square shapes. She even remembered how to make a cheesecake with soft mascarpone cheese and broken-up biscuits.

She brought the new bakes over to the counter to sell.

52

"That looks delicious," said Basil.

A toddler and his mum were waiting to buy some cookies, but when the rocky road appeared, the little boy reached out for a piece of that instead.

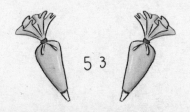

"It *does* look delicious," agreed his mum. "May we have two pieces, please? How much are they?"

"You can have them for free if you tell me how it tastes — *honestly*. I've made it without a proper recipe."

The woman squinted at the rocky road and took a bite. Her son watched and then did the same.

Both of them chewed and swallowed, and then their faces broke into wide smiles.

"Yum-mmy!" the mother said.

"More!" cried the toddler.

Ellie relaxed. They clearly liked what she'd made, even though it was without

Victoria Sponge's help. She'd tried her best and it looked like it had paid off.

The woman laughed. "He loves anything chocolatey. Chocolate biscuits. Chocolate milk. Warm cocoa . . ."

Ellie's eyes opened wide. "That's it!" she exclaimed.

"*What's* it?" said Basil.

"What's what?" the mother asked.

"*Miaow*," Whisk added, just to join in.

"The final ingredient for Talia's cake," Ellie told them. "It's cocoa powder!"

She turned and ran back into the bakery kitchen. Adding four heaped tablespoons of cocoa powder to the mixture, she stirred it thoroughly. "There!" she said.

She lined two cake tins with greaseproof paper and then buttered them, dividing the mixture equally between the two.

"That looks great, Ellie," said Basil.

"But where are you going to cook it?"

Ellie pulled a face. Victoria Sponge had told them they couldn't use the ovens without her supervision – it wasn't safe. But there was *one* place she could do it. Ellie didn't want to, but it was her only option.

"I'll have to use the ovens at Scrudge's Bakery."

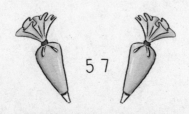

Chapter 4

Holding a cake tin in each hand, Ellie pushed open the door to the Scrudge's bakery. Whisk followed at her heels. She'd had to cover the uncooked cakes with cling film because it was still raining hard. There were even rumbles of thunder in the distance.

The smell in the shop was very unusual – even more unusual than normal. The

bakery always smelled horrible, but this time there was something chemical about it.

Her aunt was slumped behind the till when Ellie walked in. She didn't bother to say hello; instead she said, "What do you want, Shrimp?"

Ellie's plan was to put the cakes in the oven for thirty minutes, and have another look for the recipe book while they were cooking. She was sure she'd had the book last night. Now that she thought about it, the last time she remembered seeing it was just before her uncle told her about Talia's invitation.

Suddenly Ellie remembered what had happened: her uncle had mentioned her letter and she'd left the book on the table.

Ellie frowned at her aunt. "Have you seen my recipe book, Auntie?"

Mrs Scrudge smirked. "Goodness me," she said. "Have you lost it?"

Colin appeared behind his mother; he was smirking too. "Oh dear! Now you won't be able to bake any more – given that you're too stupid to do anything without it."

Ellie looked down at the two cake tins in her hands. She most certainly was *not* too stupid to do anything without the book. All morning she'd been making food without any help, and her customers had liked it just as much.

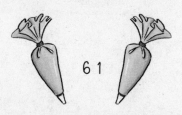

"Did *you* take my book?" she asked her cousin.

"Who? Me? I wouldn't dream of doing such a thing!" Colin placed his hand on his heart. "Be careful of accusing people without any evidence, Shrimp."

Ellie put down her cake tins – after wiping the surface with her sleeve first – and approached the shop counter. The cakes and biscuits on sale looked nice. The labels said: *Pastries for a picnic, Sandwiches for a sunny Saturday, Buns for playing board games.* These were the recipes Ellie had been looking at the night before.

The Scrudges *had* stolen her book!

But she wouldn't be able to prove it without eating one.

"Please may I try one of those?" she asked.

"Of course!" Her aunt put out her hand. "Four pounds fifty. Pay up!"

Ellie thought this was a lot to charge, but she didn't have time to argue. She got her

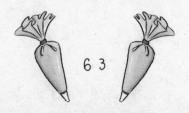

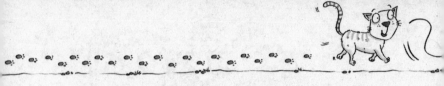

purse out of her pocket and handed over the money. "May I have a *Sandwich for a sunny Saturday*, please?" If the Scrudges *had* used the recipe from the magical book, then the rain would stop and the sun would come out. Victoria Sponge's magic had always worked like that before.

Mrs Scrudge picked up a sandwich with her dirty fingers and handed it to Ellie. Ellie inspected it – aside from the dirty fingerprints, it *did* look like a nice cucumber sandwich. She found a bit that wasn't dirty . . . took a bite . . . and . . .

. . . it was *DISGUSTING*!

The filling looked like mouldy courgette

instead of cucumber, and it tasted like compost. Ellie found a bin and spat it out.

If this sandwich had been made with the recipe from her magical recipe book, it would have been delicious . . . and magical.

When she looked outside, she saw that the rain showed no sign of stopping. It was coming down harder than ever.

Maybe I'm wrong about the Scrudges stealing my book . . . she thought.

"Sorry for accusing you," she said, feeling guilty for jumping to conclusions.

Colin crossed his arms. "So you should be." But the smirk hadn't left his face.

Ellie turned to her aunt. "May I put something in your oven, please, Auntie?" she asked.

Mrs Scrudge flapped

a hand at her, and that was all the permission Ellie waited for. She picked up her cake tins, and pushed open the door that led to the bakery kitchen.

It was even more of a mess than the shop. The floor was filthy and every surface was covered in layers of old dirt. There was mould all around the sink. This was not a healthy place to be cooking. Ellie saw that her uncle was bending over the worktop, a pile of ingredients all around him. This was strange too. He only ever cooked once they had sold the food in the shop – which sometimes took months!

"Hello, Uncle," Ellie said. "Please may

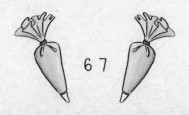

I put my cake in your oven?"

Her uncle straightened up in surprise and spun round quickly. "Oh! Hello, Ellie! I didn't expect to see you here! What do you want? To put your cake in our oven?" She could see that he was hiding something behind his back. "Umm . . . OK. Yes."

This was the most shocking thing of all! He was letting her use his kitchen without being rude or asking for anything in return.

Ellie was even more suspicious now. "What are you hiding?" she asked him.

Mr Scrudge started backing towards the door. "Nothing . . . nothing . . ." he said,

68

but his face was even redder than usual.
Then he turned and ran out of the kitchen.

Ellie wasn't stupid – despite what the
Scrudges thought: she was pretty sure that
he had stolen her book to use her recipes.
But if that was true, why had the sandwich
she'd tried tasted so disgusting?

Ellie went over to the worktop and saw

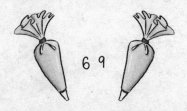

the ingredients that her uncle had been using. Instead of flour, sugar and eggs, he was using chalk, sand and glue!

Yuck!

"So that's what that chemical smell was – *glue*!" Ellie exclaimed. "And they *did* use old courgettes instead of cucumbers."

Whisk hissed in disgust.

The Scrudges had tried to save money

by using stuff they already had lying around the house.

Ellie put her cake tins in the oven, set the alarm on her watch for thirty minutes, and went to confront her uncle. But just as she reached the door, Colin opened it. He stood in the doorway, stopping her from leaving the kitchen.

"Dad told me to tell you that you have to clean the kitchen," he said, grinning, clearly happy to be the bringer of such bad news.

"He didn't say that to me!" Ellie replied.

"Well, he said it to *me*," Colin told her. "And if you don't, I'm supposed to take

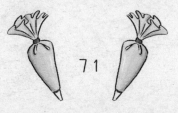

your cakes out of the oven and throw them in the street."

The cake was for Talia's birthday. It was almost midday now and the party started at three p.m. Ellie sighed. If she was going to get the cake ready and also change into her knight costume, she would need to play by the Scrudges' rules. Talia's party depended on it.

So she said nothing – just turned round and picked up some rubber gloves by the sink. She would have to clean up really quickly if she was going to get everything done in time.

Chapter 5

If Victoria Sponge had been there, she would have been able to clean the whole of the Scrudges' bakery in an instant. But even without using magic, Ellie worked pretty quickly. Whisk lent a paw too, skating across the worktops on a sponge.

Ellie glanced at her watch: five minutes

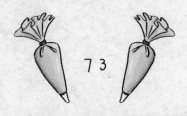

to go before her cake was ready. She ran
upstairs to get her book back.

She could hear her uncle and Colin

talking in the living room, and pressed her ear against the door.

"This recipe book is stupid. *A perfect pie for a perfect pet?*" said Mr Scrudge. "What sort of pie is that?"

Ellie had made that pie recently. It was magical.

"*A cake for a best friend,*" Colin added. "Sounds lame."

Ellie had made that too. She exchanged a quick look with Whisk and thought about Basil – her best friend – and how the book had helped her find him.

"But that's not the stupidest thing about this book . . ." said Mr Scrudge. "The

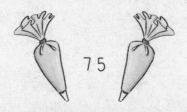

75

pages at the back are all blank – there are hardly any recipes in it."

Ellie burst in. "Give me back my book!" she demanded.

Her uncle and cousin spun round. She'd caught them red-handed.

Whisk hissed at them as Ellie stomped over to the table.

Colin moved over to stop her seeing. "What book?" he said.

"My recipe book." She pointed at it now. "There!"

She pushed past him, but Mr Scrudge got to the book first and held it high in the air.

"You said that using a recipe book was cheating," she told them, feeling very cross. "Now you've stolen it from me. *That's* cheating!"

"At least we're clever enough to steal," said Colin.

Ellie shook her head. *What a stupid thing to say!*

"Give it back," she growled. "It's mine. My dad gave it to me."

Mr Scrudge waved it around above his head. "Finders keepers."

"I don't know why you want it anyway," said Colin. "The recipes are just for horrible things like that sandwich you spat

out. It says it's a *magical* recipe book, but it's useless!"

As quick as the lightning that suddenly flashed outside, Ellie had an idea. "You're right," she agreed. "The recipe book is as stupid as I am. You might as well throw it away."

"See," said Colin. "Told you, Dad. There's no such thing as magic."

Mr Scrudge lowered the book and peered at it. "So it's worthless?"

Ellie nodded.

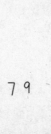

As if agreeing with her, a loud clap of thunder sounded. Whisk pressed himself against Ellie and started to shake. He was scared of thunder.

"You made *Sandwiches for a sunny Saturday*, but it isn't sunny. The book isn't magical at all."

Mr Scrudge thought about that for a moment, then shrugged. "OK," he said, and Ellie grinned. Her plan had worked. Her uncle tossed the book over his shoulder. They all watched as it flew through the

80

air and puffs of glittery dust
came out. Ellie crossed her fingers,
hoping it wouldn't be damaged. Victoria
Sponge was inside!

The pages flapped as if they were wings,
taking the book safely onto the sofa in
front of the TV. It landed with a light thud.

"Did you see that, Dad?" Colin yelped,
his eyes wide. "The book *is* magical."

Mr Scrudge's eyes were just as wide
as his son's. "We should sell it!" he said.
"A magical recipe book would be worth
millions!"

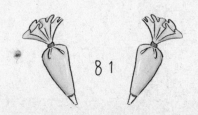

Ellie panicked. Her book couldn't be sold! She *had* to get to it before them. She was slightly closer to the sofa, but she had shorter legs.

Just then, the alarm on Ellie's watch went off. *Talia's cake!* If she left it in the oven, it would be burned.

She hesitated for a second too long. Colin pushed her aside and pounced on the book.

Ellie tried to think of another way to get it back . . . but she was out of ideas.

However, there was one thing she knew Colin wanted.

Her heart felt very heavy as she said, "Colin, if you give me the book, I will give you my invitation to Talia's party."

Colin agreed quickly. "OK!" He held the magical recipe book out to Ellie.

"Colin!" Mr Scrudge shouted.

But before her mean cousin could

change his mind, Ellie reached into her pocket and handed over the invitation. "I'm not sure why you want it, Colin," she said. "You're not even friends with Talia."

Colin frowned like he really had to think about his answer. "I want to scoff all the food at the party."

That made sense, but Ellie thought that there was more to it than that. She didn't have time to find out now. They quickly made the swap, and Ellie ran downstairs

to get Talia's cake out of the oven.

"Count yourself lucky, young lady," Mr
Scrudge grumbled as she went.

In a way, Ellie had won. She'd baked
Talia's cake *and* she'd got her book back.
But Talia's invitation said, *Please bring
this invitation to show to the butler on arrival.*
Without it, they wouldn't let her in. Ellie
wouldn't be going to the party after all.

As she dashed into the kitchen, she felt
very far from lucky.

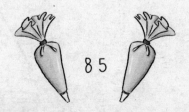

Chapter 6

As soon as Ellie was back in her own bakery kitchen, she opened her recipe book. "Victoria Sponge," she whispered, crossing her fingers and hoping that the little magical chef was safe.

The book flipped itself open to one of the middle pages, and Victoria Sponge peeled herself out.

"I'm here, Ellie," she said.

"And I'm OK." She looked very cross, though – and very dirty. The page she had been hiding on was covered in mucky finger-prints.

Victoria Sponge waved her wooden spoon over her clothes – and in a glittery instant, she was clean again. Whisk nuzzled up to her.

"The Scrudges really are disgusting!" she exclaimed. "The things they put in their cakes!"

Ellie shook her head to banish the memory of the courgette sandwich.

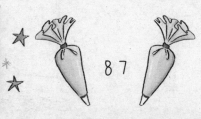

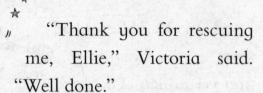

"Thank you for rescuing me, Ellie," Victoria said. "Well done."

Basil appeared beside her. "You found the book!" he said. "Where was it?"

He was dressed as a knight, with grey plastic armour and a helmet with a visor. Ellie couldn't help but smile at the sight of him. "Hi, Basil – or should I say, *Sir Basil* . . . I almost didn't recognize you without an animal on your T-shirt!" she said with a chuckle.

Basil laughed too. "I do have *this*." He turned and picked up a hobby horse that was leaning against the wall.

Whisk purred at it.

Victoria Sponge smiled. "Very good, Basil!"

"We've sold out of everything here," Basil went on, "so I had time to get changed." He looked at his watch. "There's only an hour till the party starts. We've just got time to ice the cake and get you into your costume, Ellie."

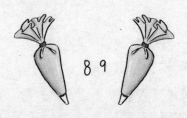

"I'm not wearing my costume," Ellie said sadly, "'cos I'm not going to the party."

Basil scrunched up his face. "Why not?"

Ellie was too sad to explain. Victoria Sponge flew up and gave her a comforting kiss on the nose.

Ellie forced a smile onto her face. "Still," she said, lifting the cakes out of their tins, "at least we have Talia's brilliant cake . . . Oh dear!"

Now that the two halves of the cake had cooled, they were not the perfect shape they'd been when they came out of the oven. One of them sagged in the middle so there was a big dent. The other sloped

90

off to one side.

"Oh . . ." Victoria Sponge said, floating around Ellie's head. "Never mind."

Ellie felt like crying. "It's because I was careless and lost the magical recipe book. I had to try to just remember the ingredients . . . and now look!"

"Don't worry, Ellie." Basil patted her on the back with his plastic sword. "It's like you always say about my cakes: they taste good even if they don't look perfect."

"But it was supposed to be *A Brilliant bake for a brilliant birthday* . . . Without the magical recipe book, I'm useless."

"You are definitely *not* useless, Ellie!" cried Victoria Sponge.

Outside, there was another rumble of thunder. "Poor Talia." Ellie slumped backwards, leaning against the worktop. "Now her brilliant birthday is ruined."

Basil looked down at his feet.

Victoria Sponge flew between them,

flapping her wings and leaving a trail of glitter in her wake. "Cheer up, you two!" she said. "We can fix this. Come on, let's finish icing Talia's cake."

Ellie knew that a lopsided cake would be better than no cake at all, so she opened the recipe book and looked for *A brilliant*

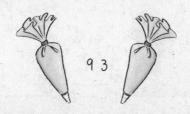

bake for a brilliant birthday. But as she turned the pages, she found another recipe . . .

"Hang on!" A smile crept over Ellie's face as an idea came to her. "We might not be able to make the cake perfect . . . but maybe we can do something about the weather."

Basil tilted his head on one side, confused.

Whisk tilted his head on one side too.

And so did Victoria Sponge.

Thunder rang out again.

"Look!" said Ellie, pointing at the page. "*Sandwiches for a sunny Saturday!*" she cried. "If we make them properly . . . following all the instructions carefully . . ."

"Not using courgettes!" added Victoria Sponge.

"I bet it will work!" said Basil.

Ellie looked down at the book, and suddenly saw a little handwritten note in the margin that she hadn't noticed before. Sometimes her dad had written notes to himself to help with the recipes.

This one read:

> Just do your best.

Ellie smiled. "Let's get started!"

The icing for the cake was made of melted chocolate and cream.

"It's called a ganache, apparently," Ellie told Basil.

"Whatever it's called," replied Basil, "it sounds delicious."

Whisk miaowed and licked his lips.

Victoria Sponge helped Ellie to melt the chocolate by breaking it into pieces, putting them in a bowl and setting this over a pan of boiling water.

"I'll make the cucumber sandwiches!" Basil said.

Ellie remembered that Victoria Sponge had made them buy lots of cucumbers at the grocer's. "Did you know this was going to happen?" she asked her.

Victoria turned on the bakery ovens. "I'm sorry – did you say something?"

Ellie saw a twinkle in her eye. The magical baker knew more than she was letting on, Ellie was sure.

Basil got out some bread and started spreading each slice with a thin layer of butter.

"Don't forget Victoria Sponge's magical baking dust," Ellie reminded him.

Victoria Sponge hovered over Basil's sandwiches, pulled a tub of her magical baking dust out of her apron and sprinkled it over the top of the bread and butter. She did the same for Ellie's ganache icing.

Once the melted chocolate had been mixed with the cream, Ellie used a spatula

to smooth a layer between the two halves of the cake, spreading the rest over the top and sides. It was still a little lopsided, but it definitely looked tasty.

Ellie had done her best, and that would have to do.

While they waited for the icing to set, she and Basil carefully cut the cucumbers into very thin slices. Then Ellie went back to finish her cake.

The recipe suggested adding a decoration. Ellie put eight candles around the edge and a simple strawberry in the middle.

"I would have loved to include a fun castle decoration on top of the cake . . ." She looked at her watch. It was twenty to

three. "But there's just no time."

Still, Ellie was confident that she'd done her best.

When they'd finished putting the sandwiches together, there were so many that they filled five boxes. They would have to use their delivery cart to take them to Talia's house.

But they made sure they left two sandwiches out – one for Ellie, one for Basil.

Ellie passed Basil his, and then picked up her own and lifted it to her mouth.

"Ready?" she asked him.

"Ready," he said with a nod.

"Miaow," said Whisk, just to join in.

Ellie took a bite of her sandwich: the crisp fresh cucumber and the soft white bread tasted amazing.

"Yummy!" Basil said.

The sandwiches were certainly delicious, but would they bring Talia the sunny Saturday that her garden party needed?

Chapter 7

At exactly three p.m. Ellie, Whisk and Sir Basil were standing at Talia's door. Victoria Sponge hid in Ellie's collar. Behind them was the cart full of boxes of sandwiches, with a big box on top, which had Talia's birthday cake in it. Whisk had tried to jump into the cart too, but there was no room for him.

Looking up, Ellie realized that the

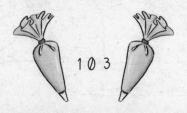

rain had eased to a drizzle. She rang the doorbell: through the stained glass of Talia's front door she saw an adult approaching.

"It must be the butler," she whispered to Basil. She'd never seen a butler in real life and felt a little nervous.

Basil looked really cool in his knight costume riding his hobby horse. Ellie looked down at herself – she wished she'd been able to put on her costume, but she had no party invitation any more, so there was no point in dressing up. She would just drop off the food and leave.

When the door opened, Ellie saw that the butler was actually Talia's mum dressed in a fancy suit.

"Umm . . . hello," Ellie stammered. "I'm Ellie, from Ellie's Magical Bakery, and I've come to deliver these sandwiches and a cake!"

"Good afternoon, Miss Ellie," said

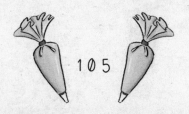

Talia's mother, putting on her best butlery voice. "And yourself, good sir knight." She bowed low to both of them.

Basil bowed and Ellie curtseyed. She couldn't help but giggle, in spite of her nervousness.

"May I take your invitations?" the butler asked. "Princess Talia has been looking forward to your arrival."

Basil handed his to Talia's mum and then looked sadly at Ellie.

"I've just come to deliver the food," said Ellie, her voice shaking. "I'm afraid I can't stay."

"What a shame!" Talia's mum exclaimed. "Are you sure—?"

"Basil! Ellie!"

Behind Talia's mum they saw a princess galloping along the hallway – Talia. Her long pink dress had frills at the bottom and bows all around the skirt. Above her

107

fringe sat a glittering tiara, and her hair streamed out behind her as she ran.

"Thanks, Mum," said Talia. Then she cleared her throat and went on in a posh voice, "I mean . . . thank you kindly, Jeeves. I shall receive my guests now." She turned to Ellie and Basil. "Please enter my palace."

Ellie could hear Victoria Sponge chuckling from her hiding place.

Talia's mum left them to it and went back into the kitchen.

Talia smiled at her guests. "We are all assembled in the garden and— Oh! I can't keep this up any more! Come and join the fun! It's only drizzling now, and you never know . . . it might clear up completely!"

"Did we do it?! Did we make the weather change?" Ellie whispered to Victoria Sponge. "Will the magical recipe make the sun come out?"

"I don't know, Ellie," Victoria Sponge whispered, but there was a strange tone to

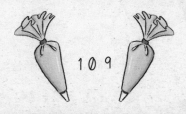

109

her voice. She *did* know — Ellie was sure of it.

"Ellie?" said Talia, looking at her properly now. "Where's your costume?"

"Well . . ." Ellie didn't know how to go on without bursting into tears. She was waiting to be told she couldn't stay without an invitation. "I don't have one," she said simply.

Just then there was a raucous noise behind them. "Howdy, partners!"

Ellie would have recognized that loud voice anywhere. It was Colin. She

turned to look at him.

Colin had dressed up – but as a cowboy, in jeans, a checked shirt and a cowboy hat, with a water pistol in his belt.

Whisk hissed at him.

"This isn't a Wild West party," Basil said.

"No it isn't!" Talia frowned. "And Colin wasn't invited anyway."

Colin cantered up the path on an imaginary horse. "Yee-haa! What are you three varmints talkin' about?"

Talia's scowl deepened. "We were talking about how I don't allow bullies

111

into my party," she said.

Colin's smug smile vanished, and he pulled something out of his pocket. "You have to let me in – I have an invitation."

"But I never . . ." Talia looked confused for a moment, then she took the invitation from Colin's hand and inspected it. She shrugged and handed Colin's invitation back to him. "You've just crossed out Ellie's name and added yours."

It was Ellie's fault that Talia had to let mean Colin into her party. "Sorry, Talia," Ellie said, unable to look her in the eye. "I gave him my invitation."

"But that's not how party invitations

work!" said Talia.

"It isn't?" asked Ellie.

"It isn't?" Colin sounded just as confused as Ellie.

Suddenly it all made sense. Colin didn't want to come to the party to scoff the food; he wanted to come because he had never been to a birthday party before either.

"I want *you* at my party, Ellie," said Talia. "And just because Colin has an invitation doesn't mean I have to let him in." She turned to Colin. "Be off with you," she said, the haughty voice back again, "before I fetch the palace guards!"

Colin's face fell. "But . . ."

113

"I can slay this dragon, m'lady!" said Basil, raising his sword and posing like a statue of a real knight.

Ellie giggled at the idea of Colin being a dragon – it wasn't far from the truth! If he was nicer to people, maybe he *would* be invited to parties.

"Oh no you can't!" said Colin. He lifted his water pistol and squirted.

Ellie thought quickly: she grabbed Basil's shield and blocked the shot. The water hit the shield, bounced off and rebounded

into Colin's face, splashing all over his cowboy outfit.

"Gahhhh!" cried Colin. "I'm all wet!"

Ellie laughed. "No one can defeat Sir Basil the Brave."

Colin scowled at them, then turned and ran back down the path.

Talia chuckled.

"I'm sorry I gave him my invitation, Talia," Ellie said, "but I had to."

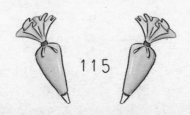

Talia gave a regal wave of her hand. "All's well that ends well, Ellie. Now come on into the garden."

"Even though I'm not wearing a costume?" Ellie asked her.

"Yes! And bring your cat too – he's adorable."

"But he's not wearing a costume, either," Ellie pointed out.

Whisk miaowed.

"I love dressing up – I have loads of spare costumes. I'll lend you one." Talia grabbed Ellie by the hand and pulled her into the house.

Ellie was thrilled. She would be going

to her first birthday party after all!

But there was still one problem, she thought: what would everyone think of her lopsided cake?

Chapter 8

Ellie and Talia held hands as they walked down the stairs. Talia had lent Ellie a beautiful gown — it was blue, with puff sleeves and ruffles all over it. Because Ellie was shorter than Talia, Talia's mum had to pin it up at the bottom, but you couldn't tell. Ellie looked like a proper princess — she even had a golden crown on her head!

They looked outside. The rain had

stopped completely now and the sun was shining brightly.

"I'm so pleased it's not raining any more," said Talia. "I wanted a sunny Saturday, and now it *is* one!"

All the guests had arrived and the garden was full.

"I knew the magic would work," Ellie whispered to Victoria Sponge.

But Victoria Sponge didn't answer. Ellie checked the pockets of her gown, but she wasn't there. She wasn't hiding in Ellie's crown, or in her ruffled collar. She couldn't have got lost again, could she?

"Are you OK, Ellie?" Talia asked.

"Umm . . . I'm fine, thanks." Ellie would have to look for Victoria Sponge later. This was a party – surely nothing bad had happened to the magical baker here.

Princess Talia and Princess Ellie made their way out to the garden. There were knights and princesses everywhere – all running around and having a good time. There was a bouncy castle at the back, and some of the guests were already jumping

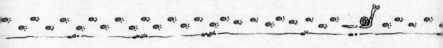

around on it.

"Come on, Ellie," said Talia. "I want to see your cake."

Ellie was worried. The party was looking brilliant so far, but if Talia didn't like the lopsided cake, that would ruin everything!

On one side of the garden stood a gazebo with a long table underneath. Talia's mum was laying out the food, including the cucumber sandwiches Ellie and Basil had made. In the centre of the table was the unopened box Ellie had brought with her. Inside it was Talia's cake, waiting for the birthday girl herself.

"Hello, Princess Ellie," said Talia's mum.

Basil bowed low. "Your Highnesses."

Talia giggled again. "Look," she said. "We even found a special costume for Whisk."

Whisk wore a bright red bow around his neck. He looked very proud as he gazed around the garden like a royal pet.

"Can we see your cake now, Ellie?" Talia's mum asked. "I've been looking forward to it."

"Talia…" Ellie didn't want her to be too disappointed when she

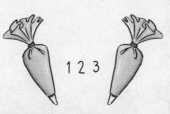

123

saw it. "I'm sorry if your cake isn't as brilliant as it ought to be. It's just . . . I found you the perfect recipe, but then I lost the book. I had to make the cake from memory." She winced, waiting for Talia's face to fall.

But instead, Talia sounded sympathetic: "Sounds like you've had a tough day," she said.

Basil nodded, which made the visor of his helmet fall down. His voice came out muffled. "She has!"

"I'm sure you did

124

your best, Ellie," Talia went on. "I know it will be lovely!" She looked at the food that covered the rest of the table. "And you brought the cucumber sandwiches too. Just like a proper afternoon tea!"

Ellie couldn't help but smile. She had done her best, and it seemed like Talia appreciated it. Ellie had made another friend today, she was sure.

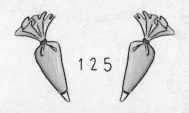

"Come on, everyone," Talia's mum called out to the other guests. "Princess Talia is about to cut her cake."

Ellie held her breath as Talia opened the box.

Talia gasped.

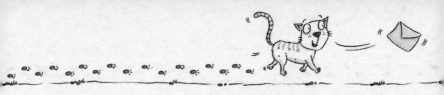

Was that an excited gasp, or a horrified gasp?
Ellie wondered.

"Look, everyone!" Talia called out.
"Look at the cake Ellie made!"

Ellie held her breath.

"Isn't it *BRILLIANT*?!" cried Talia.

Ellie let out a huge sigh of relief. Talia *liked* her cake.

Ellie peered at it – and this time, it was her turn to gasp.

It was the same, slightly lopsided cake that she had made. But instead of the strawberry on top, there was a castle, and a figurine of a princess with olive skin and a black fringe – exactly the fun castle scene Ellie had imagined. And it looked *wonderful*.

"Good work, Ellie!" came a whisper in her ear.

Victoria Sponge – she was back!

"Did you do this, Victoria Sponge?"

"I don't know what you're talking about," she replied as they watched Talia cut the cake and hand out slices to her guests. "But everyone seems to be enjoying eating it."

Ellie looked around as the guests happily tucked into her chocolate cake.

"Yum," said Talia as she took her first bite.

No one seemed to notice that the cake was a little lopsided – they were all having a great time.

Ellie realized that a brilliant birthday didn't have to be completely perfect, it just had to be a fun day with good friends. It may have been the first party Ellie had

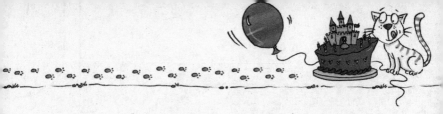

ever been to, but it was certainly the *best* party she'd ever been to.

And with the sun shining brightly, they all tucked into their sandwiches and cake. Ellie knew the day could not have been sweeter.

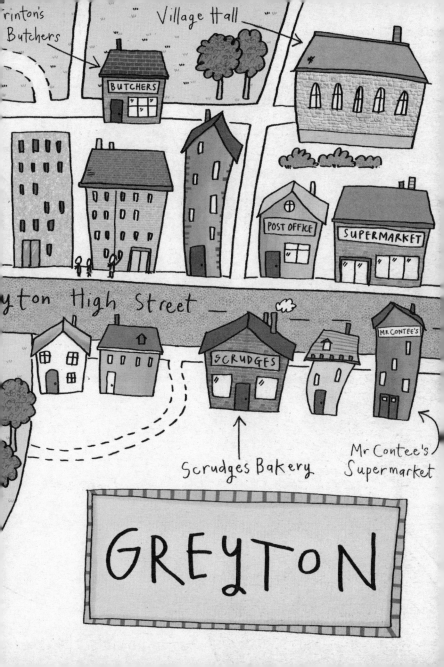

Hello, how nice to see you!

Do you like to bake?

Why don't you try out Ellie's recipe?

Make sure you always have
a grown-up around to help.

When the rocky roads are ready,
why don't you take them to the park
and have a picnic?

Happy Baking!

Victoria Sponge

Chocolatey Rocky Road Crunch

Ingredients:

250g dark chocolate

150g biscuits (any you like, but digestives and rich tea work well!)

125g butter

100g mini marshmallows

100g tasty treats (sultanas, cherries, nuts — you choose!)

3 tablespoons golden syrup

Recipe

1. Put the biscuits in a bag and mash them up with a rolling pin until you have some small and some big chunks

2. Melt the chocolate and the butter in a microwave, stirring occasionally until it is silky smooth

3. Add the biscuits and the tasty treats to the chocolate mixture, and put into a baking tin (square ones work the best)

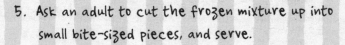

4. Put in the freezer for at least two hours

5. Ask an adult to cut the frozen mixture up into small bite-sized pieces, and serve.

Perfect for sleepovers and parties!

Read on for
a sneak peek of
Ellie's first
baking adventure!

Ellie's Magical Bakery

Best Cake for a Best Friend

♥ ELLIE SIMMONDS ♥

Illustrated by Kimberley Scott

RED FOX

Chapter 1

It was the morning of Ellie's birthday. Before she stepped into Scrudge's Bakery she took a deep breath to give herself courage . . . then wished she hadn't. The bakery smelled like old socks and soggy cabbage. *Revolting, as usual*, Ellie thought.

She looked around the bakery, hoping she might have a birthday present. The shelves were lined with week-old bread,

stale, stodgy cakes and mouldy muffins. Her uncle, Mr Scrudge, stood behind one of the shop counters mixing cookie dough. Ellie watched as he shoved a fistful of chocolate chips into his mouth, then swept a handful of dead flies off the worktop and into the dough. *Yuck!*

And there was no sign of a present.

Ellie knew very little about her mum, and her dad had died three years ago. She remembered his ginger beard, round cheeks and silly deep chuckle. Whenever she thought about him she was surrounded by the aroma of freshly baked cakes . . . not this horrible smell! Her aunt and uncle ran her father's bakery now.

They had changed the name of the shop to "Scrudge's Bakery" and had moved into the flat above it with Ellie and her ginger cat, Whisk.

She hadn't had a birthday present since.

Mrs Scrudge was slouching in a chair behind the till, her belly squeezing out of the top of her trousers. "What do *you* want, Shrimp?" she asked Ellie, straining to reach a mug of tea.

Ellie passed her the mug. There *was* something she wanted – even more than a present. She was going

to ask her aunt and uncle
for a special birthday treat.

Whisk ran over and
rubbed up against her leg.
It gave her courage.

"Umm, it's my birth—"
she started to say.

But the door to the shop suddenly
opened and a man walked in.

"Customers! Quiet!" hissed Mrs Scrudge,
and heaved herself up in her chair.

Whisk hissed. Ellie stroked his fur and
looked up to see who it was. Customers
were rare since the Scrudges had taken
over the bakery. It was Mr Amrit,

147

a man she'd seen around the village. Clearly he hadn't heard how awful the food was here.

He strode up to the counter confidently, then caught sight of the horrible-looking cakes, cringed, and held his nose.

"Hello, sir," Mrs Scrudge simpered, batting her eyelashes. "Do buy something from our delightful shop."

"Er . . . no thank you," said Mr Amrit, backing out of the door. "I've just remembered, I . . ."

Ellie went to hold the door for him — she couldn't blame Mr Amrit for wanting to leave. But her aunt lunged forward

and grabbed Ellie's arm while her uncle blocked poor Mr Amrit's exit. Mr Scrudge was huge – the size of a garden shed – with stubble on his face and neck.

"Buy something from our delightful shop," he growled. "Or else!" He put up his fist.

Mr Amrit cowered, then forced a smile onto his face. "My wife *is* partial to carrot cake," he said, his voice shaking with fear. "D-d-do you have some?"

Mrs Scrudge gave him a slice of cake. It was furrier than Whisk.

"Do you think that's safe to eat?" Ellie asked her aunt. "It looks a bit green."

"'Course it's green," Mrs Scrudge snapped. "It's Brussels sprout cake."

Ellie winced.

Mr Amrit winced.

Even Whisk winced.

Who would want to eat a Brussels sprout cake?

150

"It was *carrot* cake I was after," Mr Amrit said. "You know, with the creamy white icing—'

Mr Scrudge raised his fists again and Mr Amrit said, "But this looks nice too." He took the cake, handed over his money and hurried out of the shop.

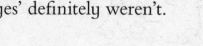

"Come back soon!" called Mrs Scrudge, then she slumped back in her chair, puffing from the effort.

Ellie felt terribly sorry for Mr Amrit. Cakes were supposed to be delicious, tasty treats. The Scrudges' definitely weren't.

She'd never dared eat any of their cakes – not since she'd heard worrying gurgly noises coming from the tummies of the villagers who had. But when Ellie was younger, her dad had let her help in the bakery. She wanted to try baking again – to make her very own birthday cake.

"Uncle," she said. "It's my birth—"

"I'm busy!" he yelled at her. But he was only busy cleaning out his ears with his finger.

"I could help you in the bakery if you like." Ellie pulled her long brown hair into a ponytail, ready to get stuck in.

Mr Scrudge turned and laughed. "Don't be ridiculous!"

Mrs Scrudge laughed too. "You are too small and too stupid to make cakes. In fact, you're too small and too stupid to do anything."

Ellie crossed her arms in front of her chest. She *was* small. She had a condition called achondroplasia, which meant she was shorter than most people.

But there was no such thing as *too small*. An ant can lift things fifty times heavier than itself. A salmon swims thousands of miles. Even the smallest birthday present can make a person very happy.

And Ellie was most certainly *not* stupid.

"But if you would like to prove you're not completely useless," Mrs Scrudge said, "go to the garden centre and get me some cement mix. I can't be bothered."

"Why do you need cement mix?" Ellie asked.

"It's cheaper than flour," her aunt replied.

"And mud is cheaper than chocolate," added Mr Scrudge.

Yuck!

"Can't Colin go?" Ellie asked. Colin was her cousin, the Scrudges' twelve-year-old son.

"No," said Mrs Scrudge. "He's out."

Ellie was certain Colin *was* out: he was

155

probably out bullying someone.

"Fine," she said. It was annoying how lazy the Scrudges were, but she was pleased to have an excuse to get away from them.

"Make sure you're back by four," Mr Scrudge called after her. "Or I'll put Whiskers in the next batch!" He threw a burned bun at Ellie's cat.

Whisk miaowed, annoyed. Ellie snapped back, "My cat's name is *Whisk*!"

"What's a whisk?" said Mrs Scrudge.

Ellie shook her head in dismay – any baker should know what a whisk was!

She held the door open for the cat as they left the shop.

Then she stumbled.

At first she assumed that Colin had left something on the ground on purpose, to trip her up; he'd done that before. But when she looked down, she gasped with surprise. There on the doorstep lay a neatly wrapped present about the size of a pizza box. It had a bow on it, the paper was covered in pictures of cupcakes with candles on, and the words *Happy Birthday Ellie* were written on the front.

"Do you think the Scrudges have bought me a birthday present after all?" Ellie wondered aloud. But deep down she knew that there was more chance of Whisk buying her a present than Mr and Mrs Scrudge.

There was a note on the front that said:

Open in secret

Ellie knew just the place . . .

Turn the page
for lots of fun
Ellie's Magical Bakery
activities!

There are still some blank pages in Ellie's magical recipe book. Can you help Ellie and Victoria by writing down your favourite recipe on this page?

Ingredients:

....
....
....
....
....
....
....
....
....
....
....
....
....
....
....

Recipe:

Ellie has baked a cake but she needs your help to decorate it. Can you help her by colouring in the blank cake below?

Ellie has lost her magical recipe book! Can you help her find it?

Quiz Time!

1. How many bags of sugar did Ellie need to buy at the grocery?

2. What was the animal on Basil's T-shirt when he was squirted by Colin's water pistol?

3. What was the colour of the writing on Talia's birthday invitation?

4. What was the final ingredient that Ellie almost forgot to add to Talia's cake?

5. What were the three ingredients Uncle Scrudge used in the Sandwiches for a sunny Saturday instead of flour, butter and eggs?

Answers: five; crab; gold; cocoa powder; chalk, sand and glue

Recipe Book Disaster

Oh no! The Scrudges have spilt raspberry
jam all over Ellie's magical recipe book!
Can you help her figure out the
names of the recipes?

STRAWBERRY CHEESECAKE

ROCKY ROAD

OATMEAL RAISIN COOKIES

CHOCOLATE FUDGE CAKE

RED VELVET CAKE

Word Scramble

Can you unscramble the names
of the characters below?

SABLI

LIELE

KWISH

ITCORAIV

LIONC

ATLAI

Spot the Difference

Can you spot five differences between these two pictures?

Hints and tips for having fun in the kitchen!

Hint: You can use lots of different treats
to make Rocky Roads - marshmallows, raisins, biscuits.
Anything you like!

Tip: Always use an apron so you don t
get your clothes dirty.

Hint: Make sure you read the recipe carefully
so you don t go wrong!

ELLIE SIMMONDS is a four-time Paralympic swimming champion and has ten world records to her name. At 14, Ellie was the youngest recipient of the MBE, and also now has an OBE – both special titles awarded by the Queen. Ellie has continued to succeed in swimming, but she also loves to bake! Working on Ellie's Magical Bakery is a really exciting new way for Ellie to pursue her love of cakes and bakes.

Ellie's disability is called Achondroplasia (dwarfism). Achondroplasia means that Ellie has shorter arms and legs than most people. As a result Ellie is a lot smaller than other people her age, but this has never stopped her from doing the things she loves the most.

KIMBERLEY SCOTT is a professional illustrator and designer. She regularly works on a diverse range of projects and loves to delve into imaginative worlds. Kimberley lives and works in London, from her teeny-weeny studio, with a constant supply of green tea and pick-and-mix sweets to keep her creativity flowing!